FISH
STORY

FISH STORY

BY
KATHARINE ANDRES

ILLUSTRATED BY
DE LOSS MC GRAW

SIMON & SCHUSTER BOOKS FOR YOUNG READERS
Published by Simon & Schuster
New York London Toronto Sydney Tokyo Singapore

SIMON & SCHUSTER BOOKS FOR YOUNG READERS
Simon & Schuster Building, Rockefeller Center
1230 Avenue of the Americas, New York, New York 10020
Text copyright © 1993 by Katharine Andres
Illustrations copyright © 1993 by DeLoss McGraw
All rights reserved including the right of reproduction
in whole or in part in any form.
SIMON & SCHUSTER BOOKS FOR YOUNG READERS
is a trademark of Simon & Schuster.
Designed by Vicki Kalajian.
The text of this book is set in Futura Demi Bold.
The illustrations were done in watercolors and collage.
Manufactured in the United States of America

10 9 8 7 6 5 4 3 2 1

Library of Congress Cataloging-in-Publication Data
Andres, Katharine. Fish story / by Katharine Andres;
illustrated by DeLoss McGraw. Summary:
When he encounters a very large fish
that agrees to grant him a wish, Craig invites him home
to meet his family.
[1. Fish—Fiction. 2. Wishes—Fiction.
3. Humorous stories.]   I. McGraw, DeLoss, ill.   II. Title.
PZ7.A5593Fi 1993 [E]—dc20 92-14677 CIP
ISBN 0-671-79270-9

For C., T., G., and W.,
with all my love
— KA

For Mrs. Dill and the
Okemah Public Library
— DM

One day, Craig sat in a small boat, thinking. He was happy, but at the same time there were certain things that he wished for—some that could be seen, others that were invisible.

He wished for happiness for his family, and for a bigger house for them. He wished for a pet donkey, for more time in the day, for sour cherries to bake into a pie, for trips to faraway places. His list was long but contained nothing urgent.

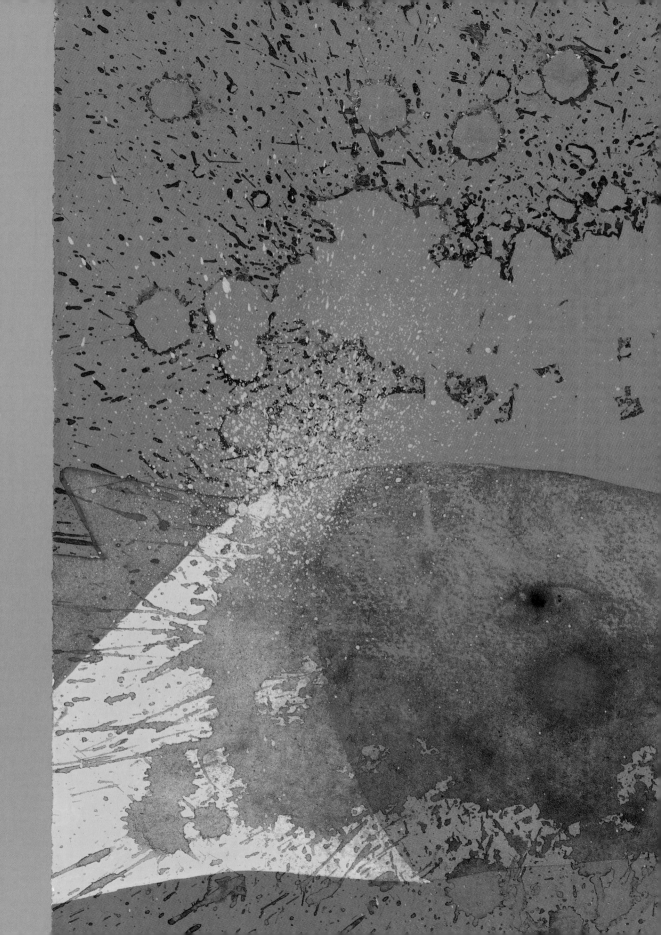

Then up from the water came a very big fish, who said, "Hello."

They introduced themselves. The fish was named Otto.

"It is an underwater kind of a name," he explained, and Craig saw that it was. "I've come because you weren't fishing," he said. "I've never liked fishermen."

Craig watched Otto, waiting for him to say more. Idly he wondered whether he would be granted a wish.

"Yes," said Otto.

Craig was embarrassed. "How did you know what I was thinking?" he asked.

"Fish know things," Otto said. "Trust me." He held onto the stern of the boat with his flippers.

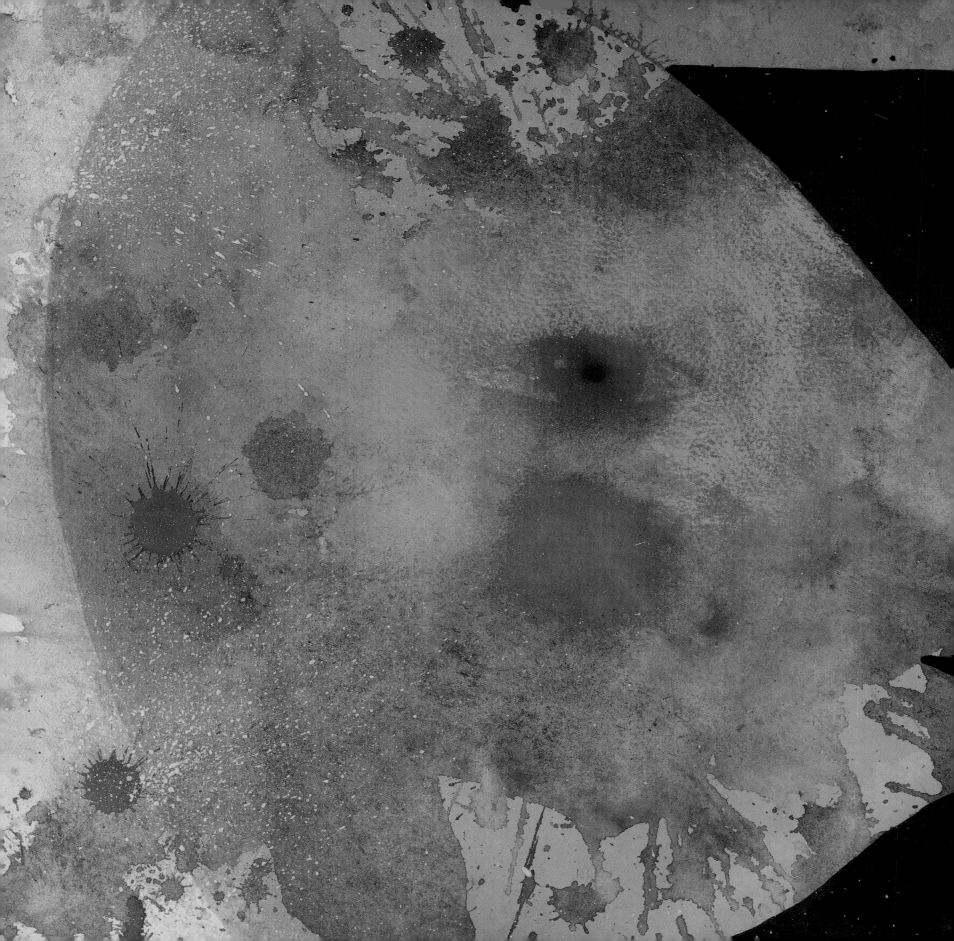

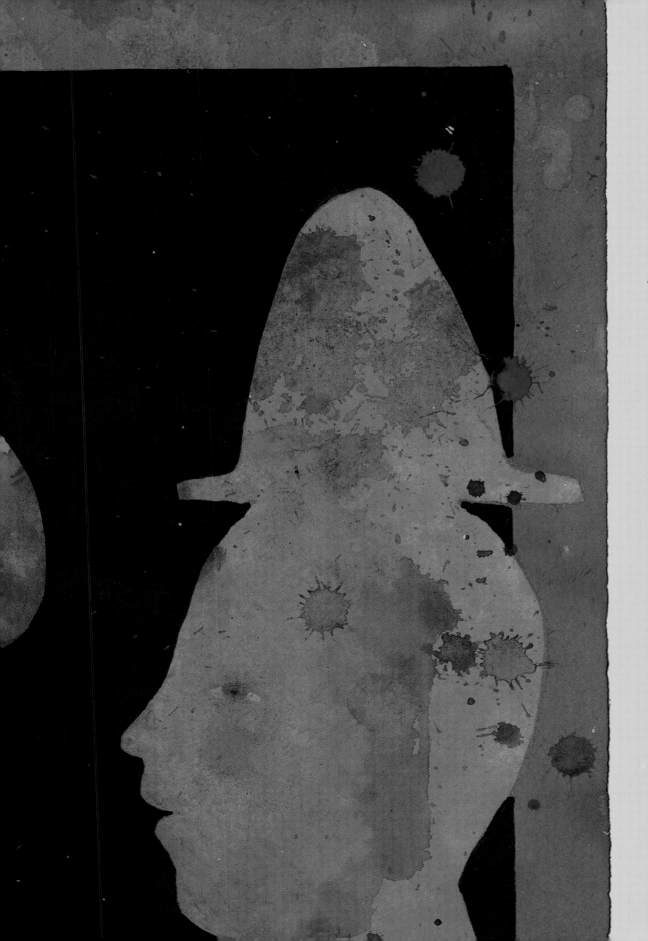

Craig said, "I've always thought that it would be best to wish for an unlimited number of wishes."

"I don't think that's possible," Otto said.

Craig looked at Otto, who slipped back into the water now and then. "Are you comfortable?" he asked.

"Fine," Otto said. "Do you need time to think?"

"I do," Craig said. "Will you come home with me and meet my wife and children?"

"I'd love to," Otto said. "I've always longed to know about dry land. Imagine how curious you'd be about water if you'd never bathed or been swimming. Sometimes I overhear a conversation from a sailboat or find a newspaper that hasn't disintegrated too much to be read, but it's not quite enough."

"I can imagine," said Craig, who swam underwater with his eyes open.

Otto swam next to the boat until they reached the shore, and then, to Craig's surprise, he proved equally graceful on land, skimming along on his tail.

In Craig's house were Ann, his wife, and their two sons, Henry and Felix. The two cats, George and Gilbert, were there, and they watched Otto with curiosity. Henry was old enough to be surprised by the fish out of water. Felix was young enough so that nothing surprised him—not elephants, human pyramids, or skywriting.

"Sit down," said Ann, wondering if she should offer Otto the bathtub. He was far too large for any pot or bowl.

"I think I can manage a chair," Otto said.

Ann watched with admiration as he bent himself into the big armchair. "Would you like something to drink?" she asked.

"Bubbly water?" Otto asked, and Ann went to get him some.

When she came back, Craig said, "Otto has offered to grant me a wish, but we need to decide what to wish for."

"A bigger train set," Henry suggested.

"I don't know," said Ann. "I'd be so afraid of making a mistake."

Felix lurched and staggered, practicing his walking, and said, "Bap."

Otto was managing his drink skillfully until Felix came close enough to tug at his tail. Some of the bubbly water sloshed onto his middle. He said, "It reminds me of home," and smiled at them all.

Henry hovered nearby. This was something he would remember for years to come.

Craig went on thinking. "What would you choose?" he asked Otto.

Otto paused for a moment and looked sad. But then he said briskly, "Fish are generally content."

"You don't dream about things?" Craig asked. He suspected that Otto was missing something.

"I dreamed of being able to grant wishes," Otto said. "I thought it would be awfully nice. Then I woke up this morning feeling particularly jolly—something was different—and I thought, 'I must be ready. This is my first try. I'm just learning how to do it.'"

"Felix is learning to walk," Henry said.

"I remember learning to swim," Otto said. "It was effortless."

Craig was wondering if he should wish a large wish for the good of the world—clean air and water, no poverty or sickness. Looking over at Otto who was intent on a conversation with Henry, he had a moment of misgiving about the extent of the fish's power.

"You're quite right," Otto said. "I don't think I can handle state-of-the-world wishes just yet."

Suddenly, Felix stopped playing and began to howl.

"He's hungry," Henry explained to Otto. He followed his mother into the kitchen to get Felix a bottle. When they came back, Craig held Felix, who was quiet again. He was watching the evening sunlight reflect off Otto's scales.

"Will you stay for dinner?" Ann asked. "Craig is making spaghetti."

BOOK HOUSE

"Thank you," said Otto. "I've often wondered about spaghetti. It seems like such a delicacy to a fish—like nondangerous worms." Then he saw the look on Ann's face and said, "Oh, I'm sorry."

Craig had come to a decision. "It's a lot to ask, I know, but what I'd really like is one wish for everyone in the family. Is that all right?"

Otto only hesitated for a moment before he said, "That's an excellent wish. Think carefully," he said to them all. "Your wishes are irrevocable." Ann said, "Can we save Felix's wish until he's older?"

"Of course," Otto said.

"I've used my wish," Craig said to Ann. "It's your turn."

"I'll wish for our own house then," she said. "An old, lovely house that a family in a children's book would live in."

"I can do that," Otto said and turned toward Henry.

"Will you come and live with us? We'll have a bathtub and a hose and a sprinkler," Henry said. "That's my wish."

"I'd love to," Otto said. "And, in fact, I'm not missing the water at all."

"I think you should still have a wish of your own," Otto said to Craig. "Do you have one?"

"Just the obvious things," Craig said. "That all the people I love be happy and healthy."

"I can do that," Otto said.

Then they all had dinner.
Felix sat in his high chair
and ate kidney beans
one by one. Otto found
a way to untangle his
spaghetti and eat it
strand by strand, and
Henry, sitting
next to him,
admired this.

When no one else was listening, Otto whispered to Henry, "Thank you for guessing my wish. I couldn't be happier."

"Me, too," Henry said.

Soon they settled in the new house, with Otto happily taking care of them all.

Three years later, Felix wished that they could eat plums and raspberries all year round and that they could take a long trip to England or the moon. He could not be made to understand that these were two separate wishes, and Otto was happy to grant them both.

The five of them had a wonderful trip. George
and Gilbert stayed home and had a peaceful
time reading, thinking, and writing postcards to
the rest of their family.